To Cliodhna with [best]
wishes. Thank you [for]
kind help, suppo[rt]
and hospitality during my
wonderful visit to Belfast.

Friendly

08.11.12

Christmas Stories

Faysal Mikdadi

Christmas Stories   Faysal Mikdadi

First published in 2012

Printed and distributed through www.lulu.com

Cover design, painting 'Beach Walk' and Author's photograph by

Faysal Mikdadi

ISBN: 978-1-291-09299-8

When Catherine and Richard were little, I used to write a Christmas story to be read to the family on Christmas Eve. Over time, this became a family tradition which was regularly adhered to.

These are some of the stories written over the last thirty or so years.

As ever, they are **dedicated** to Catherine and Richard who are now parents with children of their own.

Merry Christmas. *Christmas Ebenezer!* Christmas everyone... *and it was always said of him, that he knew how to keep Christmas well, if any man alive possessed the knowledge.*

... and *God bless us everyone.*

Faysal Mikdadi

By the Same Author

Novels:

Chateaux en Palestine, Paris, France, 1982.

Tamra, London, United Kingdom, 1988.

Return, Raleigh NC, USA, 2008

Poetry:

A Return: The Siege of Beirut, London, United Kingdom, 1983.

Bibliographies:

Gamal Abdel Nasser, Westport, USA, 1991

Margaret Thatcher, Westport, USA, 1993

Faysal Mikdadi, Born in Palestine in 1948, was carried to Lebanon where he was brought up and was given his rather unsuccessful education. He moved to Britain in 1967 and has lived there since. He is an English Literature specialist with a keen interest in the Nineteenth Century Victorian novel and in Shakespeare. His published works include novels, poems, short stories, bibliographies, educational essays and regular contributions on current affairs.

He started writing at a very early age during a turbulent and unhappy childhood. His urge to write comes from a deeply felt need to try to make sense of a disordered and crazy world and to laugh at his own rather stodgy attitudes to a much sought after quiet life. It also comes from his need to laugh at others' predictable higgledy piggledy existence and to celebrate his deep love of nature – the only place in which he sees any order and a semblance of logic.

Contents

Childhood Journey

Credit Crunch. There was something awful even in the sound of these words. They conveyed the sort of noise that real crunching makes. Like when a child steps on a small drink can hoping to crush it. And when she can not do so, she jumps on it and it crunches noisily.

And life felt a little like that crushed can of drink. Lying there with its various old colours interspersed, artistically conveying its old purpose of urging men and women to part with their hard earned cash for a ghastly fizzy drink that did them more harm than good.

Jennifer Slade felt oppressed on that cold rainy day on Christmas Eve. She drove her car through the city streets without paying much attention to anything. Her mind was elsewhere. Her job was at risk. People were simply not buying products these days. Everyone was retrenching and holding on to their money.

Christmas Stories   Faysal Mikdadi

Jennifer was driving home from work. She wondered how long she would be making this drive in the near future. Her department head had made it clear that, of the thirty people employed there, ten had to go. The first to go would be those who were office based. They were a bit of a luxury that the company could no longer afford. And Jennifer was distinctly office based. Something she had always regarded as her good luck since she hated the cut and thrust of the sales person's life.

"Hey! Watch where you're going Mrs... We wanna live to see Christmas!" Although the pedestrian's voice was loud as his fist hammered on the bonnet of her car, he had a big smile on his face. Jennifer smiled back and mouthed "sorry" without knowing exactly what it was that she had done to cause his outburst. The traffic was hardly moving. She pulled her handbrake up and removed her foot off the brake. The driver in the car behind her, a woman putting her make up on, suddenly disappeared into darkness as the brake lights went out. Her inside light came on and her face looked spectral in the white light after looking sun burnt in the brake lights a few minutes earlier. Jennifer smiled to think of the world of make belief, seeming and perception. Much more colourful than reality, she decided.

She drove slowly in the traffic congestion inching her way out of the city. What if she were to be made redundant?

She calculated that she would have about seven thousand pounds in redundancy pay. Minus tax maybe. But somebody in the office had said that you did not pay tax on redundancy packages. She made a mental note to check with her brother who, as an accountant, would know about these things.

As her car inched forward, she calculated how she would use the seven thousand pounds to make it stretch as much and as long as possible. She remembered her father telling her, years before he died, "Redundancy is not a disaster. It is an opportunity. Once you've gone through the pain barrier, you move on, have a break, refresh yourself and then make a new beginning..."

He had smiled at her little face with its huge brown eyes staring at him in that soft and gently innocent way. She sweetly wrinkled her nose at him and smiled with wide eyes twinkling at his kindly manner. Jennifer and her father had a very close and special relationship. If she ever made a success of her life, she was more than happy to give much of the credit to that lovely and gentle man who, as her father, never tired of encouraging and challenging her. As far back as she could remember, her father had been honest with her in everything that he had said. When, as a child, she fell over, he always smiled broadly at her and said, "Oh! Imagine how much less of a person you would have grown to be if you hadn't experienced this little tragedy. The graze will go in a few days. But the happy memory of the pain receding will always be with you." She never understood what he said but she always smiled happily instead of crying over her injury.

"Merry Christmas. Merry Christmas."

These merry shouts wafted through her closed car windows from people walking home from their place of work. The joy was forced because of its very repetition. It was real because each was looking forward to getting home for the Christmas break with its warm magic created on the pretence that it was for the children when it was the adults who were utterly soppy about every little Christmas tradition. The children went along for the sake of their embarrassing parents.

Jennifer laughed when she remembered how her little brother had marched into the room and asked their mother to tell him the truth. "Was there or wasn't there a Father Christmas?" Her parents had looked uncomfortable. Her father smiled at his wife affectionately and both looked at the four year old boy and clearly decided that only the truth would do. On being told that Father Christmas did not really exist but that it was a nice Christmas tradition – make belief, Richard had shrugged his shoulders and said, "Okay" as he walked out of the room, apparently none the worse for his discovery.

As her parents exchanged affectionate glances, she burst into tears. Her mother ran towards her and put an arm around her.

Jennifer had managed to say, amidst heart rending sobs, "But Father Christmas does exist…"

Her father had smiled broadly and immediately said, "But of course, my little princess, Father Christmas does exist. We know he does because we see the presents that he brings and we know that he eats the mince pies and drinks the Sherry that we leave out for him."

Jennifer had begun to calm down as she stifled her sobs and nodded vigorously at her father's words.

"And," her father continued, smiling at her. "We had to lie to Richard and tell him that he did not exist because that was what he needed to hear today. You know what it is like with little children." She had felt so grown up to be part of this momentous secret. She stopped crying.

What she did not know was her father had immediately gone off to Richard and sat him down on his little bed and told him to listen carefully.

"Now little fellow, although Father Christmas does not really exist, you must pretend that he does. Okay? You have to do that for the sake of your sister and for the sake of millions of little children who believe in him."

In later life, Richard told her that he had felt so grown up to be trusted with this special secret – in order to protect his sister, who was, after all, several years older than him.

"Jennifer! Jennifer!" The voice was coming from the pavement to her right. She looked and saw Nabil trying to manoeuvre his way through the traffic towards her car. She let her window down as he sidled up to her.

"Jennifer. I can't believe that I have met you. Unbelievable. I was wondering how to get to you. I am so busy with all those last minute shoppers and my little shop will not close till later tonight. Ah! Christmas Eve! I love it but it's exhausting." He passed her a gift-wrapped box through the window. "This is for you. Open it later when you are alone." He disappeared so quickly that, were it not for the colourful package on the passenger seat beside her, Jennifer would have thought that she had imagined the whole encounter.

She continued her slow and tortuous journey home. Classic FM was playing her favourite Christmas Carols. But she was in no mood to sing with them. Her mind twirled and reeled with numbers being divided. Seven thousand divided by three. Maybe four, or even five, months. Her mortgage was not huge and she had no debts. But then, this time of year, the heating bill will be high. Maybe they could spend Christmas in the front room and save on central heating. She could always make it a game for the children – camping in the front room.

But then her two children, Roberta and Richard, named after the heroine of *The Railway Children* and after her brother, were not responsive these days. She sighed to think of today's young children whose only pleasure seemed to be wanting things and wanting them right now. No wonder there was a Credit Crunch. People just could not keep living beyond their means.

She suddenly missed Rochester. Her husband, whose real name was John, had once told her that she was a little mad and needed to be locked up in the attic. Since then, his name was Rochester and it stuck. Rochester had worked for Medicins sans Frontiers and had been killed in Gaza during the Israeli invasion. The Israeli Government had apologised to Jennifer saying that his killing was an accident. But she knew from the witnesses whom she had met on her one and only visit to Palestine, that her husband was shot in the head trying to save a Palestinian woman from being dragged off by two Israeli Border Guards. It was plain murder. But then Rochester was a great man whose bravery was a huge source of pride to her. She had a very special place for him in her heart.

Ironically, her new boyfriend was an Israeli whom she had met in Jerusalem. He had helped her with travel arrangements and had appeared at her hotel one evening and checked that she was all right. Over the last four years, they became good friends. And Jennifer knew that she was falling in love with him. But somehow her memories of what happened to Rochester were a barrier to any more serious relationship developing and

David fully understood and kept his distant – except as a friend. The children really liked him and loved it when he visited in the summer.

As she inched her way forward she absently glanced at the Christmas lights hanging outside shops and across the road. They glistened on her wet windscreen and she could see them moving in a tinselling pattern sliding down the glass. They danced to the gentle music of Mozart's *Aria* from *The Marriage of Figaro*. Rochester used to sing it to her rather clumsily but oh so lovingly. Each little bauble of light suddenly burst into hundreds of colours and she realised that she was crying. As each tear burst out of her eye and slid down her cheek the coloured lights shook gently, burst outwards and suddenly reduced themselves to astounding clarity of vision.

Life had not turned out as she and Rochester would have liked it to. And her brave father, proud as ever of her, died with his hand in hers and a compassionate smile on his face as her huge eyes moistened during his last few minutes. So typical of him to feel sorry for her when it was he who was dying. But death had no terrors for him for, as he kept repeating, *it was a far far better place that he was going to than he had ever been to before and it was a far far better thing that he did in this life than he had ever done before.* He had said that very near his death and he twittered mischievously at his usual habit of misquoting his favourite author, Charles Dickens. Her father had indeed turned out to be the hero of his own life and no one else held that station – not even David Copperfield.

She arrived home and walked in wearily. As soon as she opened the door, her two children came walking towards her. Richard was affectionate despite his awfully grown up nine years. Roberta was much too grown up to show any affection. She nodded to her mother and gave her the usual disapproving look that she reserved for all adults between eighteen and ninety. Roberta was twelve.

Dinner went well until Roberta asked her mother if she could stay with her friend Carolyn for the week after Christmas. In principle, Jennifer had no problem with this proposal except that Carolyn lived in County Cork in Ireland. And with redundancy in the air there was no way that Jennifer could afford it. And even if she could, at this late stage and during the festive season, tickets were difficult to come by and, if available, they were too expensive.

Jennifer listened to her daughter plead and watched her sulk. She tried to recalculate the seven thousand pounds by dividing them into fewer months and, by doing that, trying to extract the price of the ticket. As Roberta flounced out of the dining room, Jennifer felt exhausted. Richard helped her clear up and he kept touching her – almost as if by accident. He was such a little gentleman.

A long time after going to bed, Richard came down in his pyjamas. He came into the front room and his mother asked if he was all right. He looked embarrassed. He held out a box and said, "You have it mum. For Bobby to go to Ireland..." and he ran out of the room and up the stairs. Jennifer opened the box and it was full of small coins. She felt her heart get heavy with regret at not being able to afford it and, yet, so light at the thought of the little boy's generosity towards his sister.

She tried not to cry. She desperately needed someone to speak to. Just to put it all in perspective. Like she used to do with her father.

She made herself a mug of tea and settled down to watch the news. The national news was all about yet another mass grave in Libya, about the Israelis threatening dire punishments for Palestinians and the gloomy Stock Market sliding into free fall. The local news was worse. It was about her company's proposed lay offs. Nothing new but seeing it on television made it an even more frightening reality.

As she turned all the lights off, she spotted Nabil's colourful package on the side. She wondered what was in it.

These late nights were her favourite times. Especially Christmas Eve when the world seemed so quiet and the weather so crisp. Her father used to carry her to the back door and they would look at the clear sky with millions of shining stars glistening down at them. Silently, they watched looking up, her father at the stars, Jennifer trying to see if she can spot Santa Claus's sleigh with its lovely reindeers. She always saw it and held on fast to her father who patted her little back as if he understood her sense of awe and wonder.

She opened the back door and looked out. Her heart filled with warmth as the old feelings came pouring into her very fibre. She held Nabil's box but did not think of opening it. As the thin film of clouds moved away from the bright moon, she could see the trees in the garden. She listened attentively to their gentle susurration which always made her feel so secure. Rochester had first confessed his undying love for her under an old Eucalyptus tree on a windy November afternoon. Susurration had become part of their feelings of love since then.

She walked into the kitchen wishing that, if only for a few minutes, she could have her childhood back. Her old special Christmas Eve treat with daddy: standing by the back door before going up to a warm and secure bed to sleep immediately so that Christmas morning would arrive quickly.

She walked into the kitchen and put Nabil's box on the table with a feeling of gentle regret at the inexorable changes wrought by time moving relentlessly forward. If only.

She opened the box. It was empty. She looked into it under the light. Empty. Silly man, Nabil had a memory like a sieve. He had obviously forgotten to put her present in the box before he wrapped it up. He would be mortified when he finds out his omission. He was one of the kindest men ever; leaving a trail of happiness behind him wherever he went.

She shook the box and held it upside down. She shook it again and golden powder floated out and trickled down to the floor. She wondered what it was as a strong deep white light shot through the back door and filled the small entrance area and the kitchen.

Jennifer stood mesmerised and a little frightened. She walked out to the entrance area by the back door and held her hand up to shield her eyes from the bright light.

Suddenly, the light faded slightly as a figure walked towards the back entrance seeming to grow in size as it approached the back door. Her heart throbbed with joy as she saw her father walking towards her.

"Hello princess. *Christmas Ebenezer. Christmas Mr. Fizziwig. Scrooge my boy. Enough work. Put all aside and make a space for dancing. Mrs. Fizziwig has prepared a feast fit for a princess.*"

Even in this improbable dream world Jennifer laughed to hear her father misquoting Dickens as he always did in life.

He came towards her holding his arms out and she fell into them and rested her head on his shoulder. She could smell his after-shave which brought a flood of gentle and happy memories.

"Oh daddy. My daddy!" she whispered remembering Bobby at the end of *The Railway Children*. "So lovely to see you."

"Lovely to see you too my princess," he said as he held her chin in his gentle hand and wiped away her tears of joy with his other hand.

"Come. Come. This is a fine opportunity, too fine to waste on tears of regret. It is not a useful emotion. We have dances to perform and we have food to eat and we have souls to make happy. Come. Come little princess."

He took her hand and led her gently into the light which softened as they walked into it. There were lots of people there. Some had been dead for years but they looked so happy and almost young even those with white hairs and craggy skins. There was music. Laughter. Tables straining under the weight of delicious food so beautifully presented. People milled around chatting noisily and laughing loudly. It was a large room, a little like a spacious barn that had been thoroughly cleaned. Jennifer thought that she could see a young Scrooge standing aside staring at his older self who, in turn, stood by the Ghost of Christmas Past looking so happy as memories of a previous life flooded into his very old and tired soul. She wondered if this were her own *Christmas Carol* experience.

Her father took her onto the floor as the music struck up. They danced with such ease as one does only in dreams. She followed his steps with remarkable facility given how clumsy she normally felt. They laughed a lot. The music got faster and faster and they twirled so fast that she thought that they might fall over.

As the music stopped and everyone cheered and clapped, they walked back towards the delicious food. Bobby and Richard came running towards their mum and hugged her. Bobby whispered, "Sorry mum. Sorry. Merry Christmas mum".

"Merry Christmas darling."

Jennifer was rearing to ask her father all kinds of questions about the after life, about Heaven and Hell, about God, about her children's future and her own future. Would their lives be all right? Will they all meet in another and better world? Is her mother with him?

Her father smiled as if he knew what was going on in her mind. He looked around and she followed his eyes and saw her mother walking towards them. She had her arms out and Jennifer walked into them and held fast on to her mother.

Jennifer did not care about asking the questions. She knew that she would regret it later. After Christmas, she will return to work, if she still had a job, and she will kick herself for not asking the obvious questions.

"But it is not important," said her father. "These are academic questions princess. The intellect is over valued little one. See the world with your heart. Be happy. You need not understand as long as you feel…"

She knew that she did not agree. But she loved his words. She loved the atmosphere. She loved the very feeling of being where she was at that minute.

"Oh dad, this is so lovely. So right. This is real life."

Her father laughed. "I told you princess. *Life's but a dream*. And this the dream of life. Shakespeare."

She laughed so happily as, yet again, her father misquoted England's second great author after Dickens. She herself was full of misquotations from the two authors.

"Dad I love your literary pretensions. I always had when you were..."

She fell silent and looked embarrassed. Her father laughed, "Alive? That was the word that you were looking for. Alive! But little Princess. I am more alive now than I ever was when I was alive in your theatre of a world. Mine is the real world where we are all eternally alive."

"What's it like dad?"

"You remember when Rochester first kissed you?"

"Yes dad," she whispered.

"That's exactly what it's like. All the time. Life's but a rehearsal that is best played without too much planning or preparation."

"Shakespeare?"

"No. My words. And mine alone."

And he looked away as the music stopped and there was complete silence in the room which started to darken slowly. The light focused on one corner that she turned to look at. Rochester stood there smiling gently as she ran to him followed by the children.

The parents held each other and their two children and stood a long time in silence.

Jennifer felt a hand on her shoulder. She looked around to see her father who pulled her towards him. As they walked off, the light spread across the room which was now empty. She looked back. Rochester, Bobby and Richard were gone. She heard the children's happy laughter coming to her from very far away. Laughter that she had not heard for so long: long, deep, throaty laughter from the heart.

Her father took her by the hand and walked her towards the tables now almost denuded of food.

"How they eat. In both worlds. Insatiable," said he laughing.

He pointed to a comfortable chair and Jennifer sat down. Her father made two coffees at the table with apparent ease and at great speed. He brought them over and handed one to his daughter. She took a sip and, although boiling hot, it did not burn her. It was perfect. Just as she liked it with four sugars. Rochester used to laugh at her taking so much sugar. He said that all he had to do was look at sugar and he could feel his weight increasing.

"Well princess, time is a-moving. I need to go back. No. No. Don't look frightened. Mine is a beautiful world. I live in a divine cottage and my two neighbours are wonderful. Dickens and Shakespeare. We get on so well. They love my adaptation of their works. In fact Dickens said that it was a far far better way that I recite than he ever did. And Shakespeare said that words are not words if their meaning be his and not someone else's. Or something like that…"

Jennifer laughed throwing her head back.

"That's better princess. Laugh and the world laughs with you. Cry and you must think that you are an American looking at his country's foreign policy…"

He moved near her and sat facing her.

"Listen princess, I feel my long journey beginning. Don't be upset about work. Everything works out in the end. Everything. That is the way of this world. Because it is preparing you for ours. Relax, take a break and make a new beginning. And let Bobby go to Cork. Ireland is beautiful. Ireland is the land of poetry. '*Riverrun, past Eve and Adam's, from swerve of shore and bend of bay, brings us by a commodious vicus of recirculation back to Howth Castle and Environs.*' See? I can do it."

"Perfect dad. You quoted Joyce impeccably correctly!"

"You can afford to because Joyce sounds like the quintessential misquotation... Must go now love. I have delivered my message. Make a new beginning. Be happy. And why don't you look at my old Oxford University wooden chest. It is a great antique princess. Like your mother and me..."

The lights went out. Jennifer was standing in the garden looking up at the sky. The moonlight streamed down so gently and bathed the swaying trees and filled Jennifer with warmth.

She walked into the house, shut and locked the back door and went into the kitchen. She still held the mug of coffee that her father had made. She sipped from it and it was boiling hot. She flinched as it burned her mouth slightly.

She went upstairs, pulled the loft ladder down and walked up into the loft. In the corner stood the wooden chest. She walked towards it and knelt before it.

She opened it. Amidst the neatly piled books there were a few files and on top of all was a folded piece of paper.

She opened it.

"Dear Princess, Nil disperandum my little one. *All's well. All manner of things will be well.* Take this wooden box to Nabil's antiquity emporium. Give him this letter as a reminder of our agreed price for this great antiquity. It is not a lot. But ten thousand pounds would help you rest, reflect and then make a new beginning. And it would pay for Bobby's trip. Merry Christmas little princess. Merry Christmas..."

31

Christmas Stories   Faysal Mikdadi

She could almost hear her father's voice fading into the
background as she sat by wooden chest.

She felt happy. She felt warm. She felt loved. She felt good.
She felt safe.

She felt. And all was well.

Christmas Eve

Dedicated to Inhabitants of Cloud Cuckoo Land

It was a dark and cloudy morning. Sophie stood by her window dreaming. She could hear her two daughters arguing vociferously downstairs.

She was too tired to reprimand them.

Across the road from her house, she could see Doc putting the rubbish bags out. She smiled affectionately at his sleeveless shirt and slippers. As if it were mid August instead of darkest winter. She could not remember ever seeing him with a coat on – even in the bitterest of winds.

Doc, as everyone mock affectionately called him, lined up the three bags neatly and in perfect symmetry – rather like his books in the library that she could see from her downstairs window. Immaculately straight and neat.

He bent down and parted the Lavender plants gently. He slowly stood up holding a black cat. He was softly whispering something. He stroked it slowly and the cat rubbed its head against his shirt.

He walked across the road and gently placed the cat on Chris's window ledge. As he walked away, he waved to the cat and whispered, "Merry Christmas pussycat". This was immediately followed by several loud and violent sneezes.

Sophie remembered that the Doc was highly allergic to cats. He stood by his car vigorously rubbing his eyes. Jenny, his wife, came out of the house. Her name had been Fleur-Jenny and she had always been Fleur. Recently, she had taken to calling herself Jenny after her little lamented late mother also called Jenny. Probably a guilty reaction at having despised her mother so vehemently in life, she was attempting, with signal futility, to love her in death.

She rushed into the house and returned a few minutes later with a bowl of water and some cotton balls. She dipped the cotton balls into the bowl and gently washed her husband's eyes. Occasionally, she stopped doing this and wagged her finger at him. He, far from the sixty year old dignified and professorial Doc, stood there like a five year old rubbing his eyes violently and utterly inappropriately under the dire circumstances in which he found himself.

Sophie saw him suddenly grab the bowl, place it on the top of his car, throw the wet cotton ball into the bushes and take his wife by the hand. He twirled her around the pavement in a mock and rather badly executed Waltz. Sophie thought that his was a rather graceful movement for a portly, clumsy, flat footed, splay footed old man. Jenny laughed and bent her head back letting her beautiful blonde hair flow behind her. He manoeuvred her to the door and placed a gentle kiss on her forehead as he propelled her into the house and quickly shut the door.

He stood by the front door rubbing his hands in glee. He walked to the bush and retrieved the discarded cotton bud. He crossed the road and placed it in the municipal bin. Then he crossed back and straightened one of the rubbish bags that had dared lean almost imperceptibly out of the straight line.

Doc stood staring at the trees across the small green. He smiled and walked across the road and back again, stepping into a little pool of water without apparently being aware of it. His walk appeared aimless but in fact, for the astute observer, he was clearly trying to create a perspective of the trees at different angles rather like an artist does with his naked model.

Sophie laughed. Doc is in for another telling off for soaking his slippers and socks. Poor long suffering Jenny. She has had to cope with this loveable fool for so long. She *would* fall for the only absent minded twit in the whole neighbourhood.

Later on, Sophie shouted at her girls to get on with it and shooed them into the car and drove off. As she did so, she saw Doc hold the car door open for Jenny. She could also see that he had changed his wet socks – into an odd pair, one black and one light blue. Jenny pointed at his feet and threw her head back in despair. He bent down as she got into the car and whispered something. Jenny burst out laughing and smacked him playfully.

He walked around the car and got into the driver's seat waving to Sophie as she drove off.

Doc sat in his favourite coffee shop staring at his Christmas list. It was covered in ticks and he looked immensely satisfied with himself. He had bought endless books for Jenny who was an avid reader. But clearly deciding that a feminine touch was needed he had bought her a beautiful little and rather dainty vase with a hint of blue and red in its very core. He was rather pleased with that choice. It showed that he was in touch with his feminine side – whatever that meant. That was what Jenny had said to him when they first declared their love. He had never quite known what it meant but, it flattered him because he despised manly men. For his daughter he had bought a gold bracelet. And all five children, his and Jenny's from her first marriage, got one copy of his latest book. He smiled to think of the exquisite cruelty of such a Christmas gift!

37

Richard, his son, had booked a holiday in Dubai with his wife Keli. They had been saving for it since almost a year ago. The collapse of the British pound had meant a loss of almost forty per cent of their holiday savings. Doc had decided to give them a thousand pounds in United Arab Emirates Dirhams to make up the difference. It would be an early thirtieth birthday present for both as well as a second wedding anniversary present. They were going to Dubai just a few days after turning thirty.

He delighted to think of their faces as he handed over a thick envelope. His son would give him a tight bear hug and say something about loving his big man. Keli would hug him in her special gentle way and whisper something adorable. Last time she had said, "I'd kill anyone who hurts you…" He was touched but bemused. Why should she say that? Did she know something that he didn't? And then when he said something to shock her, which he loved doing, she would put her fingers in her ears and sing "la la la la" as loudly as she could to keep his rude language out of her lovely little world. He smiled to think of how he had once decided that he really should come down from Cloud Cuckoo land occasionally.

But then, why should he? He was happy there.

He walked into the bank and queued calmly behind impatient customers. Cashiers looked harassed. Jenny sat behind a new cashier gently whispering instructions and encouragement. The young man looked terrified.

Jenny looked exhausted and kept clutching at her upper chest. She did that whenever her Asthma played her up. She looked up and saw Doc. Her face lit up and she smiled broadly whilst mouthing 'I love you' at the same time. He was looking right at her and yet did not respond to her smile. She wondered what universe he was inhabiting at that particular moment. Probably dreaming of Hatta in Dubai. Something had entered his soul in Hatta and he had not been the same since then.

He was still incredibly gentle and kind. In fact, even more so. When she spoke to him on the phone last time he was in Dubai, he had said, "Give the children my love..." She almost died at this cataclysmic shift. Another time he had defended her eldest daughter taking her time finding a new job after being made redundant. When her youngest son wanted to go to the States to see his new girl friend, Doc had laughed and 'lent' him a thousand pounds. When she spent a further six hundred pounds on equipping him for the trip and said that she wanted it paid back just to guard against her husband's usual disapproval of any lack of independence in their children, Doc had stroked her cheek gently and said, "Oh, let him be. He's in love. I hope he enjoys her..." using shocking language. "When you're in love, undo your belt and look for trouble. Dive in and savour every God gifted moment of bliss. And if he hurts her in any way, I will personally break his neck".

Jenny was severely shocked. Not because Doc was recommending rabid sex. That was the norm with him despite his so called advanced years. Never seemed to get enough of it. No. Her real shock emanated from the fact that he was defending family members. Amazing development. He had always had a vicious congenital hatred of all family links. He had eight nephews and nieces whom he had hardly ever seen. One was actually living in Dubai. He probably worked with him

40

without knowing him. She remembered how he had got angry in their first year when she offered to send Christmas cards to his family. He had abruptly and cruelly responded, "Cut that trivial crap. Can't stand it". And he sauntered off into his study slamming the door behind him. She cried and he was mortified and he spent the next week doing everything for her. She preferred him when he was a little vague. Actually easier to manage than when he felt guilty and would not stop being nice.

Doc waved frantically at her from the queue at the bank.

"Ah!" she thought. "He's back. I wonder where on earth he was this time." His eyes were red and the right one looked comically swollen. Jenny smiled at his obscene pun on the word "pussy" as she got into the car earlier that morning. Thank God he was only allergic to the furry four legged variety. Although, he had been a little subdued in that delectable department since Hatta.

She wondered if he was under sugared more than usual with these endless vague moments. She decided to check with the nurse at the diabetic clinic he had recently attended and refused to talk about.

"Don't fuss old girl. Don't fuss. Men like me never die. We are immortal. Haven't you seen it first thing in the morning...? It frightens even me, its best friend!" He had laughed and returned to lining up his coins neatly, adding, "I'm not compulsive. Just neat. You kiss the left eye, then the right, then the tip of the nose, then the mouth very gently, each breast twice – one firm kiss and the other a mixed quick passing licking kiss of each nipple, then the mouth deeply, followed by the last soft kiss. There you have it, ladies and gentlemen, ten kisses precisely. Divisible by five – a favourite number of all geniuses – by two – as in the human body and soul with the soul in two each half searching for its mate, with a one and a cipher but still larger than one. Cabalistic in the extreme... Voilà!"

Jenny normally stopped listening when he shouted nonsense about cabalistic numbers and their particularly interesting influence on absolutely nothing.

Harmless eccentric, really. Occasionally a little irritating and insensitive. But makes up for it with his kindness and gentleness.

Doc took his envelope with its Dirhams bulging somewhat. He waved at Jenny and mouthed "see you later".

He walked into Clintons. He picked a blank card with a drawing of a beautiful landscape of trees. He loved trees. He regularly spent holidays in Scotland breathing in the fresh fragrance of trees. And wanted to die there.

Thirty or so years ago, Colette Buchanan took him there to meet her dad. The two men disliked each other intensely. The younger Doc and Colette could not share a bedroom because they were not married. So they used to make love in the forest. It never quite worked. He was too passionate and she was too reticent. The whole act became almost comical and somewhat too functional. A year later, they parted, both deeply hurt.

Colette died of a drugs overdose at the University of Sussex. Doc had cried bitterly on her fresh grave as he had dug clumps of earth out and thrown them at the mourners. They had let him be until he fell asleep on her grave. He had woken up at midnight and cried again.

He had not really loved her. It was the excess of youth and the tears were for his irretrievably lost innocence.

Maybe he could find it again one day. That other lost soul separated from his, throughout creation thousands of years ago.

Outside the bank, cheerful carols filled the air. Doc joined in clumsily. Lorna, an old friend was there. She walked up to him and he put his arm around her frail shoulders as they sang 'O Little Town of Bethlehem'.

Lorna had lived in Palestine before 1948. She loved it and cherished her memories of it. She had adopted Doc after

44

hearing him give a talk at her local church. She was active in her support of the Palestinian cause.

They hugged when the carol was over.

"Have a lovely Christmas. Give my love to Fleur."

"Will do, Lorna. You have a lovely and peaceful Christmas."

"God bless you."

They hugged again.

"This is heavy," said Lorna pointing to a bucket full of coins.

"Shall I carry it into the bank? Jenny could help..."

"Jenny?"

"I meant Fleur..."

"Not to the bank. To St. John's…"

"I'll take it, love," said Doc picking up the bucket with ease.

"Bless you, my boy… Bless you…"

Doc walked into the silence of St. John's Church. He stepped into the vestry and hid the bucket behind the small surplice hanging on the side. As he stepped back into the church, he let the latch down hoping that the vicar did have his key on the old strap around his neck.

Essentially, Doc was an inveterate and rather sulky non believer. It was as if God had let him down somehow and he wanted none of Him.

So, why should he feel odd checking his shopping list? Indeed, it was apt to do so for Mammon was the new god of all. And this recession showed how angry and vengeful he was: sitting there paring his fingernails and laughing at human frailty.

A sob. And another.

The sobbing came from the corner diagonally opposite to Doc's resting place.

He peered into the dimness. As his eyes adjusted, he could just discern a human form. Occasionally, the shoulders heaved and the head sank further down as another heart rending sob escaped the miserable form.

Doc took in a deep breath and got up to leave. He believed that feelings were private. Misery was private. Like intimacy. It was best enjoyed in solitude and occasionally shared only with one other. He walked towards the exit. He stopped.

He turned around and walked back into the church. He approached the sobbing form. He could now make out the head and neck. It was a woman. She looked vaguely familiar.

He came forward.

"Madam, forgive me..." he intoned gently.

She jumped up in apparent terror. He recognised her.

"It's all right, Sophie. It's all right..."

He placed his hand gently on her shoulder and softly, oh so softly, he pushed her down again.

"Sit down, my dear..."

She collapsed into the pew and, putting her head in her hands, she sobbed uncontrollably.

Doc sat beside her silently. Occasionally, he patted her shoulder almost imperceptibly.

After a while, Sophie appeared to calm down.

"Sophie, what ails you, my dear. Can I help?"

"I'm sorry. Making a fool of myself…"

"Not at all, my dear. Not at all… Tell me what the matter is…"

"It's silly. I'm just upset. Frightened. Been made redundant and money's tight."

"I'm sorry to hear it. You liked your work…"

"I know. But our order book was almost empty. They had to let me go. The girls don't know. I've been out of work for over two months. I get up every morning, dress for work and take the girls to school. I've looked. There is nothing. Nothing."

And she broke down crying again.

"Calm down my dear. Calm down. Listen, my school, you know where I'm Chair of Governors. Well, we're looking for a part time Clerk. Could you help us? We would be so grateful. I know that you're a bit of a wizard with technology and all that. It's not

49

much I know. You're above that kind of work. But for now. As a filler. You know, you would be doing us such a favour..."

"Are you sure?"

"Oh, please say yes. We are desperately in need of help. I was just on my way to the employment agency to see if they could help. But we would rather have you with your excellent qualities. And we know you and like you."

"All right..." she whispered as she wiped her eyes.

"Good show. We have a meeting on 4 January. It's at 10.30 a.m. Gives you the chance to do the school run. Then I could meet you for half an hour to brief you on the work... What do you think?"

"Thank you..."

"Good. Well! That's settled then… Let's talk about more cheerful things. Are you off to Scotland to stay with your parents for Christmas?"

As soon as he had asked it, he knew that he had done wrong. What an insensitive oaf!

She lowered her head.

"Of course. Of course. Sorry my dear… Listen, I wonder if you could give me a lift home. Jenny needs the car."

"Oh, yes. I'd love to…" she said eagerly.

"You're too kind. First you help us out at the school and now you offer an old chap a much needed lift. Well, you've made my day, my dear…"

"Shall we go?" She asked.

"Would you give me half an hour, my dear? I need to see the vicar and then we'll be off... Tell you what! Meet me at Amici for coffee in half an hour... No, forty minutes..."

"Of course..." she said rising.

"See you in a while," he shouted as he ran out of the church.

He phoned his school's headteacher, told her that he had just decided that their current part time Clerk was being asked to do too much. That she needed support. That he knew a perfect part time Clerk. Vast experience. In fact, he had just appointed her. And he told the head to have a Merry Christmas. And he rang off.

The headteacher smiled at his breathless discourse. She was used to his odd calls. Most people shopped on impulse. Her kindly Chair of Governors dispensed kindnesses on impulse.

He ran into the post office. He asked for two hundred pounds.

"No make that five hundred..." said he as he urgently threw several five hundred Dirham notes into the tray.

"Have you just come back from the UAE, Doc?"

"Yes. Dubai. Lovely holiday. Yes. Please hurry, my dear. Urgent and all that..."

He pocketed the five hundred pounds and ran out. Leaving his briefcase behind.

"Rob! Put the Doc's briefcase in the storeroom. Jenny will probably come in for it after Christmas. He'll be upset. He's got his Dickens's *Christmas Books* edition in there..."

"I'll drive over to his place and deliver it," answered Rob. "My mum lives down the road from him..."

As coffee was being served, Sophie sat quietly being stared at by Doc.

"Now, listen my dear…"

"Yes, Doc…"

"Listen. This is for you. Get into your car. Fill it up. Go home. Pack a few things. Take the girls to your parents in Scotland. You can call at Gould's and get some presents. They do a gift wrap service. Free of charge. If you go now, you could be in Scotland tonight. Go. Go. Go…"

Sophie opened the roll of money and stared at it. She looked up at him.

"Are you a believer?" She whispered.

"No my dear. Only we are responsible for making sense of our lives. And this is my way, dear. You have helped me understand why we should love each other and create threads between us whilst living and letting live."

"Your reward will be in Heaven…"

"No, my love. My reward is already in here..." he said as he clutched his heart.

"You're not of this world, Doc..."

"No, I'm not. Jenny is always saying that I live in another universe. Cloud Cuckoo. It's beautiful there. Really beautiful. We love freely. And we care. And we leave each other alone and never judge. You would like it there. You must visit one day... Merry Christmas, my little love... Merry Christmas..."

Christmas Shadows

Christmas Eve. The first snowflake flutters. Dark skies shrink the streets. People come and go. Their steps are purposeful. Bags full of Christmas shopping.

At the best of times, Royal Wootton Bassett High Street feels enclosed. Shutting the rest of the world out. Self sufficient little market town. Its people happily ponderous. Its ethos full of colour and silence. Except for certain times of the day.

Morning in Wootton Bassett is always busy. The town's little arcade fills with people early. Some appear to be racing to get to Liz's coffeeshop first. The best coffee in the world. As for her cheese on thin toast: it is a miracle of crispiness, taste and comfort. No matter how the town's folk race to get there first; no one beats Peggy. Since her hip operation, she is invariably there first. The town crier follows on soon. Full of wonderful stories of overseas army service. Soon after arrives the school inspector. Always carrying a novel under his arm. Practising the sort of fiction that OfSTED likes publishing. Each and every one of Liz's customers is a unique and wonderful eccentric.

Eccentric certainly. Wonderful? Robert wasn't so sure. With the accumulated wisdom of his eleven years on this little planet called Wootton Bassett, he had decided that most people were bores. Especially adults. They really got on his nerves. The way they spent hours sipping their coffees and puffing on their repulsive cigarettes. The way that they always had something to say. Even worse, the way that they always asked about school. Who gave a damn about school? St. Bartholomew's Church of England Primary School was all right. But really, there were other infinitely more important things happening in Robert's young life than to worry about his school. He and his friends had affectionately rechristened the school replacing the letter 'B' in St. Bart's with an 'F'.

But then Robert had a little problem. Actually a host of little problems. Indeed a legion of big problems.

He was the product of child centred education. So he was self centred. He was the product of the Thatcher generation. So he was acquisitive. He was the only son of a one-parent family. So he was spoilt rotten. He was very bright. So he found ingenious ways of how not to do any work at all. He had a pretty little face. So everyone did everything for him. He was a weak character. So he followed the herd and was often little short of baa-baa-ing like the good sheep that he was.

And he was surrounded by adults who were too busy to give him any time. Too acquisitive themselves to give him any real care. But they gave him every little gadget that his heart yearned for.

His room had a television in it. A video cassette player in it. A computer in it. A game boy, a Sega, an electronic chess game, a host of electrical and electronic board and other games. A radio. A cassette deck. A CD player. Endless videos, CDs, cassettes. And many new glossy straight-backed books that shone off the makeshift bookshelf. Bran new books. Wonderful little worlds that his vessel was too rotten through ill use to heave forth to explore. So they remained shiny and impressive.

Robert was pig ignorant. He wore his ignorance like a badge of courage. Proudly. Like the true sportsman that he was. But then he wasn't really a sportsman because real commitment was too much like hard work – even on the field. But football was a way out of doing any learning work. Now, that really was boring. But then, adults around him accepted it when he said that he couldn't do his homework or that he couldn't read because he had football practice, because he was sailing, because he was playing rugby and so many other games.

Of course, Robert did not know any of this. Because the adults around him lied to him and told him that he was everything that he wasn't. And lacking all childlike curiosity, which was still-born in him or which, some would unkindly have it, was strangled at birth, he never asked about anything. So he remained blissfully ignorant. And egonorant.

And this Christmas Eve was no different to any other. Boring. Boring. Boring. Except for the endless presents that would be arriving tomorrow. He had compiled a lengthy Christmas present requirements list. He made it a very long list. With many misspellings to break every adult's heart and wallet equally. More an outrageous wish list. And he knew that every one and every single item would be bought for him. These then could join the endless unopened boxes lined on his shelves: glossy little plastic covers invitingly glistening at him every evening. But getting off his bed, switching the television off and opening another box was much too much like hard work. So there they remained waiting for the annual clearup when mum would dispose of them to some charity where, poor boys, with no television to watch, were more than happy to receive them.

Arriving into the steamily fragrant home, he left his mother to carry the huge amounts of shopping and ran off to do what he did best. Watch television. Robert was hooked on his television. He couldn't give it up. He had got so bad, that when he had to brush his teeth, he ran to the bathroom, got the toothbrush with some paste on it and ran back to his room to brush his teeth badly while staring at the screen. Even though he had rotten teeth. But then he did not care for his teeth much so they rotted. He did not care for his brain much either.

And the brain needs regular brushing. Daily. Or it will eventually cause you pain. That is if it worked sufficiently for you to recognize the pain in the first place.

And his poor mother. She worked so hard that she never had a minute to herself. Robert was a kind boy who meant well. He would have really liked to help his mother with the household chores. But it was well nigh impossible to do so. Television programmes followed one on the other with such rapidity that there really was little option but to lie on his bed and continue watching. Occasionally, when his mother was unreasonable and insisted on homework being done, he would sulkily trudge through the work. He could do it best while staring at the television screen sideways. He made a few errors but then, what the heck; mum always corrected his work for him anyhow. Occasionally, he found time to have a bath during the commercial break. Indeed he had perfected his ablutions to fit exactly within a break. His homework within the break. His Christmas cards to endless aunts and uncles within the break. Christmas cards were a necessary evil since on them were predicated the endless presents arriving from all corners of the UK.

Occasionally, his overworked and pale mother would shout out, "Five fives Robert?" And he would remain silent a while and then shout back, "twenty!" "How do you spell 'auntie' Robert?" The answer reverberated across the small house, "A-N-T-U-I, mum." "Good boy."

Mum had wagged her index finger at Robert for so long and so hard that she had developed an extreme sensitivity at the tip of the finger. That made it almost impossible for her to push the off button on the television set without excruciating pain. So the set stayed on.

Robert often fell asleep on his bed. And tonight was no different.

A particularly loud commercial entered his dreams of sporting glory and television world. He knew that nothing worked as well to rejuvenate his mum as Oil of Ulay. Or your money back. Half sleepily, he tried to work out how a customer could get a bottle, use half of it and send it back with a picture of grand dad showing that it had had no effect. And your money back. Then he could get a second bottle and do the same. He could make a fortune like that Soros fellow that his mum was always on about.

"Twenty-five!" He shouted as he woke up feeling clammy and a little ill. The television screen had two people doing something odd. A nurse had a man tied up on a doctor's couch and she was doing things to his thingy. Robert stared uncomprehendingly and wondered why the man looked in such pain. The woman was laughing or crying.

What odd creatures adults were.

The man screamed in a strange way and looked in extreme pain. Robert felt frightened and jumped out of bed. He ran to his mother's room as he did almost every night. Usually because he had an upset tummy (Monday night), a bad cramp (Tuesday night), a headache (Wednesday night), a sore finger (Sunday night). He was always fairly well on Friday and Saturday nights. Thursday was football training day and illness would have been terribly inconvenient.

Mum's bed was empty. He ran back to his room. The man on television was sitting up on the edge of the couch holding the nurse to him. They were laughing. The commentator said something about their "love map being perverted" and Robert wondered why television had a geography programme on so late.

The house was silent. Robert stood still trying to listen out for his mother. He wondered if she had fallen asleep on the settee. She had done that a lot recently since her boy friend went off with Alison. Mum kept saying that Alison was a bitch young enough to be his daughter. But she expected that she was willing. Yes, she was probably willing. Robert wondered if his mum's funny boyfriend had gone off with her because he too was willing. Mum said that Alison flattered him and made him think that he was as young as she was. But he wasn't. He was a fat slob. And she always looked sad when she said that.

Robert heard a noise in the kitchen downstairs.

"Mum? Mum?" No answer. He heard the noise again. It sounded as if mum was doing the washing up or maybe she was having a midnight feast.

"Mum?" He shouted at the top of his voice. He put into his voice as much terror and pain as he could possibly do. Usually that got his mother running up the stairs immediately. Followed by a hot water bottle, a drink, Disprin, Calpol, Flanagan, favourite teddy bear, fluffy tigger and a frozen pea bag.

But no one came up tonight.

He walked down the stairs slowly whimpering, "Mum? Mum? Mum?" and still receiving no answer. He heard a man laughing in the kitchen and wondered if mum's boyfriend was back. He hesitated outside the kitchen door. He wanted his mum but knew that he shouldn't go in. Last time he walked in he found his mum lying on the dining table with her boyfriend leaning over her. They said that she had a nasty spot on her inner thigh that he was examining. Robert did not feel comfortable because the lights were out in the kitchen and mum had told him to go back to bed. And then she followed him with the usual host of emergency treatment things.

"Come on in Robert. Come on in my boy," said a jovial voice from the kitchen. It wasn't the boyfriend.

Robert walked into the kitchen.

A remarkably handsome young man sat at the top of the table. All the lights were out but Robert could see him quite clearly. He had a little shining light that surrounded him and whichever way he moved the light moved with him.

"Hello Robert."

"Hello."

"Come on in and sit down a minute or two." The young man lounged in his chair and appeared so relaxed. So happy. Not a worry in the world. Just there.

"Who are you?" Asked Robert.

"I am the spirit of laziness come to see all the boys on Christmas Eve. I look in to see what they want for Christmas."

"And then you come back with Father Christmas and leave them their presents. Right!" Shouted Robert excitedly.

"No, afraid not. I look at their list and then I do nothing about it."

"Why not?"

"Can't be arsed actually. Boring. Boring. Boring. So my boy: What do you want for Christmas? Hey?"

Robert started to recite his list. This took him about half an hour. He knew it item by item. Which was a great achievement especially as his school was particularly worried that, for the last three years, he had been unable to memorise his times table because he had a very poor memory. He recited on and on and on.

The young man yawned every minute or so and appeared to be staring up at nothing in particular. As Robert recited away, the man aged before his very eyes. His hair fell out. His ears grew long and craggy. His nose slowly became bulbous. God, thought Robert, he is becoming ugly. And Robert, not having many social skills, stopped reciting and started staring.

A gruff voice lurched from the virtual monster before him. "What ya lookin' at? Hey? Don't you recognise me?"

"No."

"No what, you little ill mannered child?"

"No ... sir... Sir".

"Not sir. I am not a man. I am not a woman either. I am a childish idea, see?"

"No...sir..."

"Stop calling me sir, boy. Come here."

Robert was frightened to move. But he could not help it. He walked towards the terrible creature – for it wasn't really human. It held its chest out and pointed at its huge number of medals. Robert peered and tried to read. His teeth ached but he tried to read: "Medal first class for spectacular ignorance". "Ignorance conference 1944". "Ignorance revisited 1988". "Ignorance first prize – 1 May 1997". "Joint ignorance-laziness gathering – DfEE 1998". "Ignorance – Millenium Dome 2000". "OFSTED accredited inspector – 1993".

Robert smiled and said, "Don't tell me. You're the spirit of ignorance? Right?"

"I don't know."

"What are you doing here?"

"I don't know."

"What do you want?"

"I don't know."

"Oh for God's sake don't you know anything?"

"I don't know. I read The Sun sometimes. Occasionally I'm made to read articles by Chris Woodhead and Tedd Wragg in the TES to keep me going."

"What's the TES?"

"I don't know."

A little tear trickled down the creature's ugly cheek at the mention of the TES.

"Why are you crying?" Asked Robert.

"I don't know."

"Is it because you're ignorant?"

"I don't know. What's the day today?"

"Friday, sir."

"Oooooh! Friday. TES day. Oh God!! Help me please. I can't read."

And he burst into tears and sobbed loudly. Robert felt sorry for him and wondered what he could do. The creature lay its head on the dining table and sobbed uncontrollably as the lights went out.

71

Robert froze for a minute. It was pitch dark. He felt his way around the kitchen feeling for the light switch. He found it.

As the light came on he looked towards the chair at the head of the table. Sitting there before him was – no it couldn't be. Impossible.

It was Father Christmas. No. It wasn't. It was Jesus Christ smiling at him as he did out of all those Christmas cards. No, on second thought, it was not Jesus, it was Eddy Murphy. Ginger Spice. Alison. His mum. His aunt. The apparition kept changing at great speed. Flickering. Appearing. Disappearing. Appearing again with a new face. It was enough to make you feel dizzy but Robert was used to it. It was fast moving, changeable, incomprehensible like the flickering screen on Euro Trash. He liked that programme so late at night. It was full of boobies and bums and funny things. My mama says life's like a packet of condoms. You never know what flavour you're gonna get. Robert wondered what flavour had to do with condoms. He knew that they were little balloons that men used to stop babies. His dad had once filled one with water and it exploded in the garden. Dad was a teacher. He was in charge of the PSHE programme at his school.

"Hello Robert." The flickering image smiled and its face changed again. So many faces that Robert did not recognise. There was one he knew. Kennedy. Shot in Israel in 1956. Another one. Martin Luther King. Shot in Kosovo by Saddam Hussein. And another one. What was her name? She was a French scientist who died in an atomic bomb in her lab.

"Hello, sir... madam... sir... sir...How do you do?"

"I am doing fine, Robert. I always do fine." A young Tony Blair smiled and was immediately replaced by an even younger Margaret Thactcher.

"Who are you?"

"I'm the spirit of hope. Your mother and your friend."

"You're not my mum."

"I could be." Smiled the new so beautiful face.

"Why are you here?"

"To give you a vision of hope my boy. Come. Hold my hand."

He slipped his hand into the spirit's and they were somewhere else. In the country. Green grass and an endless carpet of bluebells stretched before them. A man was sitting before them with a child on his lap. The child could hardly have been more than four or five. They were reading a large book together. The child was pointing to the pictures and saying something. The man laughed and hugged the little one.

"Who are they?" Asked Robert.

"Don't you recognise him?"

"No."

"It's you Robert. You in twenty years. With your little child. And you are wondering why you did not work at school. Wondering why you spent all the time watching television, playing sports and not doing anything that you had to do. And it's too late. Like everyone before you by the time you discovered your mistake it was too late. And now you are desperately trying to make sure that your little one has a better chance."

"But I never had a dad to give me a chance..."

"Don't make excuses Robert. We can all find reasons why we shouldn't bother. What happens to you is up to you. You can't spend the rest of your life blaming your parents for your failures. Think about it. Think hard about it. Do you know my boy that you spend only an hour and a half out of every ten hours of your life in school. The rest of the time is yours. Completely yours. Don't you want to make something of yourself?"

"But what? What can I make of myself?"

"Whatever you want Robert. Whatever you want. Nothing is impossible if you want it badly enough. Nothing. And nothing, of course comes of nothing. You must make an effort. Think about it my friend."

Robert realised that they were back in the kitchen and he looked down at the hand holding his. He felt sad but strangely hopeful. He couldn't understand why. The hand in his was a woman's now and he liked it. He squeezed it and it squeezed back. He looked up at his mother sitting at the head of the table.

"Are you all right sweetheart?" She asked.

"Yes mum. Just had a funny dream."

"Come up to bed darling. Come on pud." Said his mum walking towards the cabinet by the sink. She bent down and picked a few things up.

"Mum?"

"Yes my little angel?"

"I'm all right, mum. I do not need anything. Put it back please."

His mother looked at him and smiled.

"I will be up in a minute to see to you, my sweetie."

"Mum?"

"Yes, little fellow."

"Call me Robert, please."

"Yes... Robert my..."

"Good night mum. Sleep well."

"Good night sweet... Robert."

"Mum?"

"Yes Robert?"

"I love you."

"I love you too Robert."

An Indian Christmas

This was going to be the best Christmas ever. Leyla was going to get everything on her list. A modest little list because Leyla was a modest little girl. Dad had said that it was all right that Christmas fell during Ramadan this year. It did not matter. Mum, Dad and Leyla were still going to have a tree. Lots and lots of good food except that the family was going to eat after sunset because Mum and Dad were fasting. On Christmas Eve actually. Then, after dinner, Leyla was going to stay up a little later than usual to open her Christmas presents.

And no school. That was the best bit. Not that Leyla disliked school. It was only that school was miserable in the winter. It was always dark in England and Leyla had never got used to it after living most of her life in Yemen where the sun shone so brightly. And during the day so hot and during the night suddenly so cold. But it did not matter at night because Leyla's bed was warm and cosy.

79

Dad was a teacher. He worked with children who did not speak English. They needed his help because he spoke Arabic and Urdu. Leyla thought that her dad was very clever. He read a lot. And some of the things he read looked so beautiful. Such lovely little shapes that she could make no head or tail of but they seemed to move across the page in such an easy going friendly sort of manner. Leyla knew how to write her name in Arabic although she always forgot to put the little dots and squiggles in the right places.

Dad had taught her to write her name and to turn it into a picture of anything she wanted. The best one was turning it into a graceful swan with a long undulating neck ending the name on the left side of the page.

Leyla's mum and dad wrote articles and did lots of translations for schools. She was very proud of them although some of her teachers occasionally made her feel a trifle odd when she showed them how to write her name in Arabic. They always looked at her with amazement and said things like, "I can't do that. That's too difficult". But of course it wasn't. They were just being silly. She didn't think that it was difficult when they wrote their names in English backwards. And sometimes what they wrote didn't look anything like the sound of their name.

Dad was expecting a phone call from the TES, whatever that was. They were doing an article on home languages. Leyla couldn't work out what a home language was. Did people speak something else at home and Arabic everywhere else? Maybe they spoke French at school like that student from Cardiff.

Dad said that if the TES called she must take a number so he can call back. She was ready with pen and paper. Mum was reading The Jerusalem Report by the front room fire.

The phone rang and Leyla jumped up. She picked up the receiver, pen poised over paper. No daddy was not at home she informed the caller. Who was it please? And she wrote it down as the Editor in Chief gave her the number.

She was excited as dad came in. Running up to him, she gave him a hug and told him that she had the number given to her by the Indian Chief. Dad laughed and she looked at him admiringly. Maybe dad taught the Indian Chief English on Monday evenings. Did they sit on the floor smoking a pipe? Did the Indian Chief talk in a deep frightening voice? She knew that he lived at the TES somewhere. He must have, because mum always said that the TES was all smoke and no fire.

The fire in the front room was wonderful. It occasionally crackled but the bit that Leyla liked most was the endless movement of the flames. Little hands that outstretched as if trying to escape their very life giving force. It was too much for them. Occasionally, a little face appeared and mockingly shifted and moved before the outstretched arms replaced it. One face stayed a little longer and did not appear to move. Its large yellow eyes stared at Leyla earnestly. She felt frightened. Maybe it was the Indian Chief. It grew and grew and came out of the chimney alcove. It hovered before Leyla a while and then appeared to sit on the floor. Impassively, the outstretched arms stopped waving and rested on the large bright yellow blubbering body.

The face smiled almost imperceptibly and Leyla smiled back.

"Hello," the face chirped in a quiet voice. It couldn't be the Indian Chief. His voice was so quiet. Almost like a little girl's.

"Hello," replied Leyla gaining confidence.

"Hello," said the face again.

"Hello," answered Leyla. "How do you do?"

"I do fine, thank you. And you?"

"Fine," said Leyla wondering who says 'I do fine' these days. "Are you the Indian Chief?"

"Indian Chief? What Indian Chief?"

"The one from the TES. Do you want to talk to daddy? Shall I call him?"

"No, Leyla I want to talk to you. I want to tell you a story for Christmas."

Leyla sat up in her chair and got ready for the story.

The one who was not an Indian Chief started talking in a quiet voice. Leyla had to strain to hear him. She was aware that even the bits that she could not hear she could somehow understand. He started.

"Ahbal lived in a very nice and quiet oasis along with his old parents, his wife and his children. They all worked hard to make ends meet. But they were happy. And Ahbal, everyone said, was a very nice father. In fact, the old ones said, there were so many nice people, so many nice trees and water wells in the oasis that it should be called Niceland. But the young ones thought that was silly.

One day Ahbal was climbing a tree to gather dates for the evening meal. He was getting tired of dates. He kept thinking that it would be nice to have lots of delicious foods. The sort of

84

food that Fatoush, the caravan leader, told him they served over in a place called Damascus. In that place they had all the water they wanted. They stopped work at five and they all went home. They ate rich food with fresh vegetables.

Ahbal came down from the treetop. He put the basket full of dates near the well and sat down to have his lunch. After lunch he lay down for a sleep. But he did not sleep for long. He was woken by a terrible roar coming from behind one of the sand dunes. He got up and walked over to discover what the noise was.

Lying on the ground there was a most beautiful lioness eating a big piece of meat. Ahbal, not to be frightened easily, came forward for a better look. The lioness roared again and shook her non-existent mane. "What do you want?" she roared. Ahbal was fascinated. "You talk?" he asked. "Of course I talk. What a stupid question!" Ahbal stared at her and admired her beauty. "You are so strong, so beautiful. Where do you come from?" The lioness looked up and smiled, "I come from beyond the sea at the end of the desert," she replied gently. "I am looking for a husband."

Ahbal thought how beautiful it would be to have her for his wife. She was strong and would fetch good food. He forgot all about his wife and children. "I will be your husband," he cried.

"You can't. You haven't got a tail."

"I'll get one," shouted Ahbal running away to fetch it. Fatoush sold him a beautiful tail. But the lioness said, "You have no mane." So Ahbal waited for months while his hair grew long. The lioness thought it lovely. "But your teeth are not sharp," she objected. Ahbal had them filed and sharpened. Now he could bite a desert fox in half. So he returned to the lioness with his new tail, long hair, and sharpest teeth. The lioness was very happy. "But you must have the skin of a lion," she told him. So he went and bought one from Fatoush who thought that he was going mad.

That day he married the lioness. He left the oasis, his parents and his wife and children to go over the sea. He did not feel sorry for his wife because he had forgotten all about her.

When they got to the other country where all the strong lions and lionesses lived Ahbal felt very happy with his new appearance. He liked his new tail, his new skin, sharp teeth and beautiful mane. They arrived at the big forest where all the other lions lived. The lioness roared out to tell the others of their arrival. They all came running to welcome them.

When the lions got to Ahbal and his wife they stood staring at them with angry eyes. "He is not a real lion!" they roared. "He is now," said Mrs. Ahbal. "He is one of us. He is just like us." But the others were angry. "He is not!" they said. The lioness told them all about Ahbal and about how hard he had worked to become a lion. But they were still angry. "Throw her out of here. She broke our rules by bringing a lion man in. Throw her out. Let us kill and eat him."

They all pounced on Ahbal and started tearing him to pieces. His wife the lioness was thrown out of the territory. Ahbal screamed as he felt the first bite that took off his tail. "No! Please don't hurt me. Let's go away somewhere else. Oh! It's like a horrible nightmare. Horrible nightmare. A nightmare!"

"Nightmare! It's a nightmare! Wake up Ahbal. Your heavy lunch gave you a nightmare. Time to go back to work!" Fatoush was shouting.

As the fiery narrator finished his story the face wriggled, moved and dived into the chimney. He gave off an intense heat and made Leyla very hot.

"Leyla. Leyla darling," said her mother. "Time to wake up sweetheart. You mustn't sleep in front of the fire like that."

Leyla opened her eyes to hear her father asking to speak to the TES Indian Chief. She felt relieved that all was normal again.

"Christmas tomorrow," whispered daddy holding the telephone receiver away from his mouth. Leyla smiled back at him.

The Fractured Comb

Edinburgh! Christmas 1980. A delightful place. A warm time.

Edinburgh! So supremely civilised. Aloof. Grand and secretive; she takes in only those who are steeped in centuries of culture.

I must admit that when I first got the job I felt somewhat nervous. I had always lived in the country and the idea of moving into a city was truly frightening. My family and I braced ourselves for the big day. After all, the prestigious University of Edinburgh had offered me a two-year contract as a "creative writer responsible for engaging students in first hand experience of the craft of writing". A good salary, generous free time and a little office all to myself, well, not quite all to myself. Somewhere there had been another modestly successful writer who was to share my two years. Richard was his name – and his game? Scum! No, I am overreaching myself. Let me start again – this time without intruding on the narrative.

90

Richard wrote fiction about what he termed sarcastically as "the lower orders". He drew his inspiration from places where most of us would be ashamed to be seen. He would claim that such places contained real life. It was a favourite thing with him to poke gentle fun at my children's stories (where my success was not too immodest).

"My friend," he would say with that idiotic leer which amused me so much. "My friend! Life is not all meadows and greenery. You walk home through the park every day. You lock your little door and contemplate your family: protected and secure. You're neither, my friend. You are as fractured as any of us".

Needless to say I took all this for exactly what it was – nonsense. I know a little tramp who regularly knocks at my door asking for money. I always give him a cup of tea and we have a little chat at the door. Oh yes. I have seen so-called Life with a big L. In fact I have always tried to reflect it in my children's stories – especially in the illustrations which I always did myself.

One nice Friday in March I walked across the park feeling particularly good. Richard was not coming in that day since he had decided to explore whatever it was that he needed to explore in order to find inspiration. I had decided to spend that day putting the final touches on a little story I had composed – for my daughter actually. There. I have let my little secret out: my little one was my inspiration in these matters.

I had been working on a little story called "The Rabbit's Warren" (hugely successful since). But I was not in luck that day.

Richard was sitting in the office frantically busying himself with clearing a space upon his desk. As usual, he had used my immaculate corner wherein to pile up all his rubbish. He looked up at me and leered idiotically. I started putting all his rubbish onto his desk. He smiled encouragingly.

"I thought that you would be observing Life," I said as sarcastically as I could.

92

"I will, my friend, I will," came his reply. I did wish that he would not keep calling me "my friend". It made me feel so uncomfortable. In my family we tended to keep our feelings to ourselves for reasons that are too complex to go into here.

I sat at my desk and started to revise my "The Rabbit's Warren". I would have got on much better without Richard whose phewing and humming (and smoking) were getting on my nerves. I eventually plucked up enough courage to remind him that Friday was a non-smoking day as per our agreement at the beginning. He leered at me.

"Have lunch with me," was his only response.

I was about to make the excuse of urgent work at hand when he interrupted me saying, "Come on my friend, we'll eat on the way home. You always finish early on Friday."

"All right". I had intended to stay on late in order to finish the story before the weekend. I thought that if I were to have lunch with Richard then I could pretend that I had forgotten something and thus return to our office after he had gone home. That would give me the office for the entire afternoon and for part of the evening. I had no need to return home early that night since I had informed my wife that I would be composing during part of the evening.

I spent the morning preparing for my afternoon stint. Richard managed to clear his desk – if one calls piles of paper on the floor a clearing process. Midmorning, he asked me if he could take a look at my little story. I have never suffered from authorial vanity so I let him have his wish. He sat back in his armchair reading with a very serious look on his face. Now and then he smiled as if approvingly. I must admit that this reaction pleased me a little. He made only one comment during the actual reading when he told me that Mrs. Bunny reminded him of Linda (my wife). I was very pleased since I had, in fact, modelled my heroine upon my little wife.

"Do you like it?" I asked him, annoyed at my trepidation.

He replied in a very serious tone of voice. "Oh yes, my friend. I like it. "And I felt annoyed even more by his serious reply. It made me feel uncomfortable. I felt like a child being patted on the head. I did so wish that he would not call me "my friend".

We spent the rest of the morning working quietly as was the rule for Friday. We had to have those rules since Richard and I were of such different habits. Without the rules (initiated by myself) we would have had absolute chaos. Generally speaking Richard did not infringe too many of our rules except in the business of smoking on non-smoking days.

As usual I jumped at the sound of the gun. I never understood why after so many months in Edinburgh that gun still made me jump.

"One o'clock!" shouted Richard. "Time to go". We left.

We emerged onto South Bridge and turned into Chambers Street. This was a favourite walk of mine. I had often headed towards the pub in George IV Bridge but never got beyond

Chambers Street. I got waylaid by one of two things. I would invariably end up in the Royal Scottish Museum where I would spend my lunch break watching people from one of the upper balconies. I took great delight in looking into the little pool of water whenever people got too much for me. The school parties usually made my day. I enjoyed following the children and listening to their amazed comments and sometimes to their mischievous ones. Either the Museum or, if I walked on the other side of the road, I would be invariably waylaid by one of my several acquaintances at that University we held in such deserved contempt, Heriot-Watt. We would then repare to The Quill where a small drink and a little sandwich went a long way towards making our discussions interesting. I was safe from any possible meetings on that Friday.

My friends at Heriot-Watt disliked Richard intensely. I always found that a source of embarrassment. Nevertheless, Richard used to ask for it. He would go out of his way to make them feel uncomfortable by questioning anything that they might choose to say. Most unpleasant.

As we arrived at the junction that connects Chambers Street with the Bridge I started to turn right heading towards The Quill, as was always my habit.

"Where are you going, my friend?" Richard stood outside the Bank of Scotland as if he were about to consult a tourist guide. "Not to the old place please. Come on, my friend, let's take a break from Heriot-Watt. Like a Tower of Babel meeting all those language people."

"Where do you want to go, then?" I asked apprehensively. "Not to the Student Centre I hope!"

"No, my friend. I know of a great place that would suit you to the ground. Right down to the ground."

I did not like the sound of that. "Right down to the ground" would invariably mean "down to earth" with Richard. But, anxious to get rid of him – I turned round and walked in the opposite direction. Perhaps it would be the Greyfriars Bobby. I liked that place. In fact, I had written a short story about the subject and surrounded it with all kinds of realistic little touches from the great legend (for legend it must be otherwise it could not work).

We passed the Greyfriars Kirk which reminded me of the country church near which I had lived all my life. I got a strong urge to pop in for a visit – but feared Richard's reaction. Suddenly, as we passed the Game Shop and as I looked into the window registering the possibility of buying the little one a little something for Christmas, Richard said, "Yes my friend. I do like your little story". I laughed and replied attempting to hide my annoyance, "I am not so sure that I like this 'little' business…"

"Why not, my friend? We must label everything. Otherwise where would we be…? Let me test you…" My heart jumped into my mouth because this introduction was always the inescapable prelude to one of Richard's funny and questioning moods. "Let me test you… How would you label those people walking around and about and so on…Now you tell me. How would you do it?"

Richard stopped outside a somewhat dingy looking pub named Sandy Bells. He would always stop in the middle of the street to ask one of his searching questions. I stood facing him conscious of the fact that we were creating a slight obstruction for other pedestrians who would look at us impatiently as they circumvented us.

"Why Richard. Just ordinary people who are popping out for lunch and looking forward to a quiet weekend with their families. They just want to get on with the business of living – if old Thatcher would allow them, that is!" I added by way of relief for Richard was beginning to annoy me. I wished I were in The Quill with old Hugh towering over his pint, Jerry biting the last remnants of his finger nails, Henrik ogling out of two thick lenses, and Martine smelling so sweetly of old French newspapers. Alas, this was not to be. Anything to get rid of Richard.

"No my friend. No." He spoke impatiently as if exasperated with a child who refuses to understand what is so obvious to his parents. "No, my friend. They are nothing of the sort. They are fractured personalities. Fractured. Badly so."

"By what?" I asked in order to keep him talking.

"Come in my friend and I'll buy you a drink. We shall discuss this over lunch."

To my great discomfort he walked into the Sandy Bells.

There was no escape. Even that was a great price to pay for getting rid of Richard. I only liked my local. I disliked all other pubs.

The world we entered was a different one to that which we had left. It was like walking into the wardrobe in Lewis's novel – except this was a Narnia without a benign Lion. This was not Edinburgh. It was – I could not tell – it was Richard's idea of Edinburgh.

The place was almost empty. An old man sat in the middle of the bar. He had a long white beard and seemed badly in need of a bath. Over his left eye the eyebrow had been singed and there was a deep red mark that gave him a permanent squintlike expression. He seemed to be making faces at me. Mocking me and my clean overcoat. He was too far gone in his drink to care much about our entry. Richard bought a pint of bitter for himself and an orange juice for me. We shared a packet of peanuts and another of crisps.

"Shall we sit here, my friend?" Richard indicated a built-in bench near the door. I agreed – thinking of my ultimate quick exit.

"Strange that this place should be so empty during lunchtime." I spoke by way of saying something.

"Pubs open all the time in Edinburgh. More civilised than your lovely England my friend. It helps. It helps."

"It helps with what?" I asked.

"To mend fractures..." Richard looked at me mockingly. He smiled. I turned and looked at our old and drunken friend. He was lolling his head from side to side as if in tune with some music that only he could hear. Now and then he would open his mouth in a horrible grimace that seemed to go well with his singed eyebrow.

It was as I watched him that I noticed his small dog. He was emaciated in a way that I had never seen in any living thing in my whole life. His owner obviously spent every penny that he could lay his hands on to buy his drinks and consequently could not feed the poor dog. The horrible living death walked up and down the corridorlike pub as if in search of something that his life depended on. He most probably was: in search of some scraps to eat. He reminded me of my daughter when just born.

One side of the pub was the bar with various bottles badly arranged against glass, mirror and several yellow advertisements. The other side was all wall and window with the built-in benches. In the middle was the main standing area covered in cigarette ends, spittle, and spilt drink.

The dog sniffed at everything around him. Now and then he would stoop and bury his nose into some revolting corner. It was out of one of these corners that he emerged with a dirty and greasy comb in his mouth. He walked back towards his master and sat at his feet. He examined the comb. He licked it. He bit into it. He pushed it with his nose. He talked to it. It was a bone. But it was without taste. He picked his ribs and skin as if about to lift a massive weight. He took the comb back to where he had gotten it. Eager for something, he burrowed further beneath one of the benches and came out with a paper tissue. He walked back and settled at his master's feet. He went through the same process with the tissue that he had done with the comb. The tissue was returned to its hiding place beneath the bench. The comb emerged again in between the dog's sorry teeth. Settled at the old man's feet he proceeded to make another very thorough examination of the comb. In his eagerness to sample its delights he broke it. This seemed to fill him with great pleasure as he started to dance around it nudging it vigorously in an attempt to break it completely into two pieces. For a split second he turned his back to me and I

103

could see his orifice – dirty and pathetic. It reminded of the time when I found my wife sprawled out on the bathroom floor crying hysterically after... I stood up to leave.

"Wait my friend. I haven't finished my drink."

I sat down again smiling feebly.

"Interesting place hey? Ten minutes a day keeps the shrink away..."

The pub was filling up with people. The old man suddenly let out a strange cry. In response the dog walked up to him and sat at his feet very quietly. The old drunk kicked him viciously. The dog squealed, moved away and returned to sit at his master's feet.

A fat man walked in and looked around as if in search for someone. His eyes rested on me and I thought that he was about to say something. He did not. He walked up to Richard and said, "Where do you come form?"

Richard's face turned a little pale. He looked up at the fat man and replied, "That depends. Why do you want to know?"

"You look familiar to me, that's all."

"No, my friend, cannot be. I'm Turkish you see."

"So was my grandmother. Turkish too. Sorry to disturb you." He walked out. I noticed that his flies were undone and that he did not seem to blink.

"Do you know him?" I asked.

Richard smiled as the colour returned to his face. "Never met him before in my life. Another fractured personality, my friend."

"Fractured?" I laughed. "More like smashed to smithereens."

"And where are we going from here, my friend?"

"Why back home of course." I lied.

"Yes I know that. Across the park. You might pop back to the University," he leered in that horrible way. "But I mean where are we *going* from here?"

"Home – or the University…" I persisted stubbornly.

I looked away as if greatly interested in the interior of Sandy Bells in order to shut Richard up – at least for a while. He still had a third of his drink to go. I tried to do a quick mental calculation as to how long a third of a pint would take to drink. I did not have the courage to leave. I felt as if I were glued to my seat and that to get up would incur the most nasty kinds of displeasure. I sat staring at people around me.

The whole place felt like Aladdin's cave with the forty thieves and without any chance of boiling oil. In front of me stood a man with no front teeth whatever. I felt the cold air to my right. I looked round. A young man – well dressed and obviously well off – popped his head in. He withdrew quickly. The toothless man shouted, "He-ya Jimm-ay gummon in. Gumm back!" He looked around him for a reaction to his utterances. No one said anything. People carried on talking to each other. A boy passed before me with half a pint in his hand. His other hand held a pretty girl with very high heels and very green hair. I noticed a spot on her left cheek. It was ripe for squeezing. Looking away in embarrassment, I spotted a middle aged and middle sized woman with large breasts come forward to whisper something to her friend at the bar. He kissed her gently. She reminded me of Martine – except she was not so clean. Our friend, the old man, was looking at his hands with a great effort as if trying to read small print.

"May I join you gentlemen?" A youngish man with a very red nose and seemingly very scrubbed face stood in front of us. I removed my empty glass from the bench. I was about to move Richard's cigarette filled bag of peanuts when the man said, "That's all right, mate. Leave it." And he sat on it. I felt the cigarette ash silently crunch beneath him. Richard, as usual, dived into the conversation by asking the man what he did for a living. The man replied quietly and with a heavy accent. He had his back to me so I did not hear him.

"We are teachers," said Richard to the man.

"Well – yew dew 'ave you wer-rk cu' ou' for ye…"

"We try to," I replied – not understanding a word that he had said.

He and Richard talked for some time about various things. At one point the scrubbed man held out his arms and revealed a horrid red patch that had swollen into a bluishy liquidy bag.

"Fractured…" he explained.

Richard looked at me with a twinkle in his eyes. "Did you hear that my friend?" I nodded. "Our friend here's fractured…" Richard's twinkle turned into something inexplicable – but certainly nasty – as he rolled his eyes like a dervish. I remembered my daughter having that first fit during our fateful holiday in Switzerland. Meningitis.

I stood up.

The scrubbed man smiled at me. "You're not going mate are you?" His accent disappeared.

"My friend is no drinker or lover of pubs," said Richard apologetically.

"I have forgotten something at the University."

Richard rolled his eyes again.

We had never gone back to Switzerland after her illness.

I turned to walk out when there was a deafening cheer from the customers. I turned round to see our old friend the drunk standing on a stool in the middle of the narrow pub.

When he opened his mouth I could not believe that such a ruined thing could sing so beautifully. This was obviously a daily occurrence as the customers all continued to chat amongst themselves once the cheering was over.

The drunk sang a Scottish song that I did not understand – but it moved me. Slow tortuous chagrin. I forgot all other noises.

The little one was singing 'Baa baa black sheep' when the fit came…

I walked up to the little dog and patted him. He looked up at me with his huge eyes. He did not dare move. I stroked him gently. He felt exactly as he smelt: defenceless.

Edinburgh! So supremely civilised.

Prince Street. Like the Champs Elysees is Paris. I remembered Martine and her French evening at Heriot-Watt. My first contact with French speaking people after the accident.

I wished we had stayed in the country and not come to Edinburgh. Eden-bur-ugh – so charming. Sophisticated. Chic.

Richard stood up and said good-bye to the scrubbed man.

We left the pub.

"Well my friend? Be seeing you then…"

"Huh? Oh yes. Monday."

He looked at me. Coming very close to my face, he whispered, "Are you all right?"

What an odd question to ask in the middle of the street. Of course I was all right. Just thoughtful.

"Ah!" he leered at me. "Thinking of the finishing touches. Thinking of your "The Rabbit's Warren", aren't you my friend?"

"Ah... Yes. Yes. Rather troublesome this revision business... Makes you want to change everything."

"But you can't, can you my friend? Well! Be seeing you." I watched him as he walked away form me. I could see him entering the park. He walked with purpose. His every stride had an irritating confidence to it.

I was in no mood for revision. I entered the newsagent's to buy some Kit-Kat for the little one.

I did so – so very much – wish that he would not keep calling me "my friend".

What's in a Name?

Jerry Polinger Carlton was a perfect deputy headteacher. Popular, funny, personable and kind, so everybody thought the world of him. Whenever the Curriculum Committee met, JPC provided nibbles and hot drinks. Occasionally, being a great wine connoisseur, he also provided the latest plonk. Autumn was a special time when the Beaujolais Nouveau arrived. JPC made the darkening evenings light up with friendship, happiness and laughter, for he was funny, was old Jerry. Very funny. And much agenda work was covered under his benign chair – even towards the end of these meetings when Ruth, the wide eyed and beautiful assistant headteacher touched JPC's thigh, squeezed it gently and asked him if he wanted to finish the 'neauvolais boujeau'. It was such a shame to waste it. Yes. Much good work went on under his chair.

And the jokes. There was not an occasion when JPC did not have a wonderful line to throw out. Like that time when Jonathan Craft, a remarkably limited second deputy, objected to a very angry parent being very angry after his daughter lost part

113

of her little finger in design technology. Oh, the finger puns. Can't quite put my finger on it. Get your finger out and do something. Don't point a finger without proof. And then Craft ponderously and irreverently told everyone that the girl's father was a banker by trade.

"Cockney rhyming slang, I assume," said the witty JPC. Meanwhile, a surgeon, more talented than Craft, managed to sew the little finger back on. And by and by, as much else in education, the finger somehow muddled on to some usefulness.

Jerry Polinger Carlton was a perfect deputy headteacher. Popular, funny, personable and kind, so everybody thought the world of him.

Everybody, that is, except the headteacher Martin Fiddle. A superb thinker, good curriculum planner and clever academic, Mr. Fiddle had the emotional intelligence of a newly born kitten. Vulnerable, easily hurt and blind. Known as BOSS (bums on seats stupid), he was held in wondrous and awesome contempt by all teachers. JPC listened to their complaints. JPC gave them tea and sympathy (and, occasionally, wine). JPC agreed with their judgements of little fat Fiddle and often provided them with various ammunition to help them damn him utterly.

And damn him they did. For one fine late September morning, Mr. Martin Fiddle, B.Ed., M.Ed. fell thoroughly dead. And the sombre atmosphere could hardly disguise the bubbling brook of happiness in the staffroom. And the jokes were good. But then JPC was on top form. And in the top job.

When the LEA adviser sauntered into the staffroom after a long and hard day of interviewing four candidates (one black male, one white apparently indeterminate of gender, one female and one JPC) and announced that JPC was the new headmaster there was an earth shattering cheer. Not even Maggie Leavis, the most ardent feminist, noticed the 'master' in headmaster; they were so happy to have JPC in post.

Next morning, Jonathan Craft, condemned to deputising for the rest of his life, quietly and sombrely read a statement from JPC:

"My Dear Colleagues. No doubt you would have by now heard of my elevation to the House of Lords. I will ask you to bear with me as I shall go into purdah for two or three weeks in order to do some strategic thinking and planning.

These are exciting times and we believe that there is much to do.

I shall keep you as informed as my leadership position allows doing. We shall certainly touch base soon. Meanwhile, keep up the Sterling work".

There were a few titters at the mention of the House of Lords. A few less at the mention of purdah and a confused and quizzical silence as to who the 'we' were.

Two weeks passed by followed by a half term. And Christmas was not too far off.

After half term, as was customary, staff gathered in the staffroom for the morning briefing. Jonathan Craft rather inarticulately asked them to "listen up guys" as an introductory to JPC's entry.

The man who entered was dressed in a very expensive looking pin striped suit, bran new shiny black shoes that clicked and clacked impressively on the wooden floor. He had a large handkerchief hanging magisterially out of his top pocket. His hair was lolled upward and backward in an imposing bouffant that added several inches to his diminutive figure.

JPC was a born again headteacher and, were it not for his voice, the staff would have thought him a newly arrived visitor from outer space or from a spinning New Labour politician's office.

"Good morning colleagues," he said loudly and with all the authority of his shiny bran new appearance. "We are looking forward to transforming this school. Our 33% five GCSE grades A*-C will be 70% in two years. Our budget deficit will be a surplus in two years..." His eyes looked through the new Calvin Klein glasses and surveyed the troops. Putting the four fingers of his left hand gently into his jacket pocket with the thumb hanging out impressively, he raised his right hand towards heaven in a Kennedyesque gesture that would have brought tears to the shocked eyes around him.

"Colleagues," he declaimed solemnly. "Give us the tools and we will finish the job. We will work hard in the classrooms. We will work hard in the committee rooms. We will work hard everywhere. We can promise you nothing but hard work and sweat. Let us, my colleagues, go forward together". And Churchill's picture behind the new headteacher's head was smiling approvingly – or ironically depending on the listener.

Teachers went off to teach their pupils. Jonathan and Ruth took a bottle of Chardonnay to JPC's newly furnished and expensively carpeted office. They presented him the bottle and welcomed him back.

JPC fell into his chair with a look of amazement – nay of horror – on his face. He eyed the bottle as if it were a weapon of mass destruction.

"Colleagues," he started tersely and angrily. His chin quivered. His right hand shook slightly. "Colleagues. Our LEA has a no drinking policy. I do not think you recognise the seriousness of your offence. To bring alcoholic beverages on the premises is a sackable offence. I shall overlook it for this time only".

Jonathan Craft, lacking, at that precise moment, the spontaneous brain electrical impulses necessary for a general comprehension of utterances and events, smiled inanely. JPC's eyes registered a distinct "you'll have to go" reminiscent of Columbus's eyes as he informed a picnicking Arawac Native American family of their sudden discovery.

Ruth, embarrassed, changed the subject quickly. "How's Kate?" she asked about JPC's wife.

"Kate? Kate?" he replied irritably. "Her name is not Kate. It's Mary from now onward. Mary. She wishes to be called Mary".

As Christmas approached, much changed in the school. Numerous committees and working parties were set up with names such as the lateral theme working party and the longitudinal planning group with an endless list of planned meetings. JPC bought an oversized black Audi that seemed to float into his newly reserved parking space at 8.40 precisely every morning. A new seven hundred page 'Manual of Indicators' was published with data on everything. JPC booked a Christmas holiday in Israel and a mid February one in Dubai. A new student report of three pages per subject was created. JPC ordered a higher chair for he seemed to grow shorter as his oversized bouffant collapsed in time to the tune of Christmas singing its carols round next week's corner.

And, of course, a new timetable was produced. The pin striped suit was beginning to appear somewhat strained as it coped with trying to envelope the energy JPC stored for future innovations.

The new timetable was a masterpiece, a pièce de résistance, a chef d'oeuvres (which is better than a masterpiece because it is French); a masterpiece of complexity.

Droves of tired, demoralised and harangued teachers gathered around it on the last day of term. The end of term bun fight had been cancelled because JPC had a flight to catch with Kate who was now Mary and may next week be Sarah of the salted visage. Ms. Heenan did not bother to look at the new timetable for she was leaving on account of a late pregnancy at 48 with a non-urgent need for a husband. Mr. Payne was giving up teaching to start a small business using hypnosis to help impotent men. And Haj Ibrahim was going to smuggle himself into the Palestinian territories for a quieter life. Ruth was at last joining her parents in Australia to celebrate their joint ninetieth and stay there to care for, and then bury, them.

But those who looked were confused. There was no key to anything. Jonathan stood by to help.

"What is CZ?" shouted one.

"Citizenship," explained Craft.

"What the hell is SLG?"

"Senior Leadership Group".

"Why is it on the timetable?"

"Blocked time for strategic planning".

"What? Eighteen hours a week. What're they planning? George Bush's education?! Improving Arabs' ability to plan for the future? Improving Israel's humanity?"

The joke was ignored. Like the wine, it was not allowed and unlike it, it grew worse with age.

"Who's CH?"

"Confederation Helvetique..." uselessly joked the geography teacher.

"Cathy Hellinger," helped Jonathan.

"But she's always been CHR...."

"We are going for two initials only except where they are the same, in which case they have been numbered in descending order of seniority," explained Jonathan.

And lo and behold, a streak of bright light came in through the steamed windows and hit upon the new timetable at the top. New red initials in bold read "JC". As the caretaker wiggled his torch about and shouted, "locking up"; Ruth said quietly, "JC. JC. JC. I can't believe it".

"Never mind," shouted Jonathan cheerily. "Never mind. It's Christmas everybody. Christmas".

At that very moment, the El Al plane was taking off from Heathrow with Mary and JC on board. The black Audi gleamed and glistened in the short stay car park. Its engine was still humming its cooling off tune. If teachers listened carefully, they might have heard it repeating over and over again, "JPC. JPC. What's in it for me. In it for me…"

The Importance of Being Earnest

Peter left home very early in the evening of 22 November 1963. This was a very important day. The Parish Council was meeting at the urgent request of Mr. Peter Auerbach of Cedar House, Bridgehead. The short agenda included a proposal by the same Mr. Auerbach.

It was also an important day because Mrs. Auerbach was preparing to chair the Women's Christmas Bazaar Committee the next day. After that, the days would fly past as she and her friends worked tirelessly to prepare the best Christmas Bazaar ever.

Every year, it was to be the best Christmas Bazaar ever. And it always was. Every Christmas.

That day had been a very busy one for Peter's wife and young daughter. They had spent the entire day visiting various wives in order to put pressure on them to get their husbands to the

Council meeting. It was imperative to get a majority of the Conservative lobby in order to get Peter's proposal voted in.

During the previous weekend Peter had spent the entire two days walking from house to house in order to get support. The weekend culminated in an address at the village hall followed by a question and answer session. There was also a dance afterwards and a good time was had by all.

While his wife and daughter canvassed, Peter carried out his teaching duties hurriedly at the small village school. He was somewhat impatient with the slower children while he ignored the brighter ones. One boy was severely told off for not knowing that Texas was in America. A map was produced and Peter angrily pointed out the vast state with his finger thumping incessantly on Dallas.

Three thirty was very slow in coming but arrive it did. Peter walked home very quickly, snatched a meal, and then left for the village hall.

He heaved a sigh of relief as he walked into the hall. There were six people including himself: three Conservatives, two Labour, and a Liberal. Peter calculated that the two Tories and himself would vote for, the Labour against while the Liberal would abstain.

The Chairman declared the meeting open. Apologies from those unable to attend were read out. Minor items were discussed and resolutions passed. The fourth entry on the agenda came up: a proposal by Mr. Peter Auerbach.

Mr. Auerbach stood up and eyed the assembly carefully for some time. He started to speak quietly but firmly. The assembled Council listened with awe. Now and again there were nods of assent from the Tory Councillors. Sometimes the Labour listeners smirked derisively. Mr. Liberal sat impassively neutral. Auerbach proposed the immediate and speedy opening of a short footpath between the Western Drive and Jonathan's village store to create a convenient shortcut for children going to school.

Auerbach's oration was impressively sober. The ensuring discussion was heated. There were shouts on all sides. The Liberal gentleman became so very heated and angered by a Conservative comment that he actually threatened to vote on the Labour side.

This was only a threat, however. The Liberal abstained. The footpath was approved by a majority of one. Mr. Davies, one of the Tories received instructions for his building firm to produce an estimate for the erection of the necessary gate leading to the path.

Peter walked home refreshed. He had won his battle. He breathed in the crisp air. He was looking forward to his milky drink as he would tell his wife and daughter about his – no, about their – triumph with the necessary flourish.

His wife and daughter were at the door. They looked worried. This was an expected state of affairs considering the momentous day. Before Peter could open his mouth his wife blurted out tearfully: "Oh! Peter! It's Kennedy. They've killed President Kennedy."

The Fourth Dimension

David switched off the radio with rising irritation. He felt angry while listening to the World Service book programme's suggested Christmas reads – barely the end of August! Some Amis poetry which he felt was an insult to human intelligence. Religious poetry of the most insular type. And a new life of Dickens to make up for it all.

It was perfectly understandable that people should keep returning to the old masters. There was nothing like them.

David's irritation sprang from the fact that his first novel, the product of endless nights of torment, had been rejected by several short sighted publishers. It lacked sufficient insularity.

David was by no means blinded to its merits. Unashamedly romantic, he had already tasted the bitter sweet meaning of success. He was confident.

He walked out of the newly bought house in the centre of the village. His wife and children were away for the weekend. A long and quiet walk would dispel any moroseness brought on by the absence of his wife on whose slender shoulder he leant heavily for support.

At the duck pond, his usual first stop, he watched the ducklings innocently and expertly paddling around. They made him think of his little daughter whose eyes always bore the hallmark of amazed innocence. He looked around, scanning the small pond carefully and systematically as if afraid to miss the slightest possible joy it offered. He noticed a girl crouching on the other side. She did not look any more than sixteen. Not quite young enough to be his daughter – though not too far off. He watched a yellow duckling trying to climb out of the water. It waddled clumsily trying to climb out of the water. It tried once more and then fell in again. It splashed a little and then paddled off as if embarrassed by its own failure.

When David looked up the girl was gone. He walked over to the other side with an unreasonable determination to find her. He realised that she had awakened some kind of remembrance within him. A remembrance – not of something or somewhere – but of some time. Sunny, parasolled, elegant and distant. He could not find her.

Walking away from the pond he was overcome with a feeling of déjà vu. He often had such feelings and, when they occurred, he cherished them. They seemed to give him a momentary time lapse which he found very relaxing. The more he fought to keep the feeling within the stronger that feeling became.

He carried on towards his usual second stop – the small brook that noisily wound its way through a maze of hedges and trees. He had often crossed and recrossed the stream with his daughter – the two of them delighting in splashing each other with water eager to outdo each the other in doing with their little lives that which mummy disapproved of: getting thoroughly wet.

The stream seemed cool and refreshing in its clear and clean snake towards somewhere. David noticed a small opening in the hedge that he had never seen before. He decided to

131

investigate. A prior knowledge of some secret place would come in handy in his next excursion with Sarah – his much belovéd four year old.

Behind the hedge lay a large field golden green with the sun. He walked across towards another cluster of trees and a small hedge at the end. His old friend, the stream, with whom he had parted company when he entered the field, appeared again. It splashed its way down several small sharp falls. It looked clean, gleaming and shimmering in the sunlight. He crossed it and entered the small cluster of trees.

A fine place for Sarah's endless fairy tale chatter.

Coming out of the small wood he was overcome by another very strong feeling of having been there before. This was the second in that day. It must have been the effect of the golden sun, the trees and the stream. Why not keep getting such feelings? After all, he had often had solitary walks. Certain things were repetitively and beautifully familiar.

He stood still on the edge of another field. In front of him, at a short distance stood a most familiar house. Large, with red inviting bricks, it changed shape and character unexpectedly. Here and there stood turrets. Windows changed from one shape to another. Through a few large windows he could see curtains and old furniture – large and solid.

The house seemed more like a human face: expressive and changing. He felt that he must go there. He walked towards the house as if drawn by irresistible mischief. That he did wrong walking into somebody else's private property he knew only too well.

Over the fence and into a beautifully cared for garden. Nothing fancy or eccentric. Clean. Supremely English with daffodils swaying their heads like careless young maidens and grass so green and childish. Round the corner he heard a clatter of plates and cups. It would never do to be caught here. Must leave immediately.

He walked round the corner. He would think of an excuse when confronted. Anything would do. He was a good talker.

Several ladies dressed in long colourful robes sat around a large table. In front of them a couple of men, immaculately attired, were chatting to each other. Children played noisily up and down the lawn. The sun seemed hotter than ever.

"Hey!" shouted one of the men looking towards David. "Where have you been?" David came forward to reply – what could he say? Yes, he had come to talk about the 'Keep Our Village Tidy' competition. As he opened his mouth to speak he noticed that a couple were slowly overtaking him and walking towards the man who had asked the question.

"Where have you been?"

"Down towards the brook," replied the new arrival as he escorted his lady companion towards an empty chair.

David stood for a while staring. He had obviously not been noticed. It was too late to retreat. He had apparently walked in on a fancy dress party – something in the genre of an Edwardian afternoon – or was it Georgian?

"Excuse me sir," he started as he walked to the two men conversing. One of the men turned around and looked at him.

"Excuse me barging in like this. I am from the..." The man walked towards him with a look of someone dreaming of far away things. Just in time David jumped out of his way to avoid a collision. There was none despite the fact that the man's arm was flung towards David.

"They can't see me!" thought David not knowing whether to be frightened or amused. From behind him he heard a murderous scream as if someone were lunging at him with a sword. He turned around. A boy was pushing a wheelbarrow with a small girl in it. Too late, he was going to run right into David who tried desperately to move out of the way. The boy ran faster and seemed to be completely unaware of David's presence before

135

him. He hit him – David felt nothing more than a tickling sensation. He looked round again and saw the back of the boy disappear around the corner.

David began to feel a little frightened. Whatever this may be it was not normal. He knew all about time lapses, the fourth dimension in time, even the most dated explanation of a vivid imagination. Whatever it was, it was unfamiliar. David was vaguely aware – as if in a dream – of his chance to find out. To investigate. He felt that he had to go back – go back where? – with some proof. Impatience overtook him. Rather the same sort of impatience he would get when hearing stories about people who claimed to have seen a ghost or an extra-terrestrial being. He felt impatient of religious zeal, of the feeble mindedness, the second hand desperate notoriety such experiences produced.

He felt embarrassed.

As he stood there staring and thinking, he noticed that the lady just brought in from her walk to the brook was the same girl he had seen at the pond. He was sure that this was the same person. Perhaps a little older but definitely it was her. It? "Not the time for literary niceties," thought David.

He was aware of being in his own study at home. He was not quite there because he could still see the daffodils. He could hear people talking and laughing. He saw books lined up against the wall in his study. All kinds of novels. People laughed. He got up and walked out to the kitchen to make a cup of coffee. He must hear what they were saying. He shook himself as if out of a sleep.

The three men were walking away. David felt that he should get out. He should go home. He wanted to do so – very much – so much that he actually pictured himself at home – making coffee.

"Hello!" said a girlish voice beside him. He turned and saw the by now familiar girl from the pond. He walked away.

"Hello!" she repeated.

"Can you see me?" he felt the question to be supremely stupid.

"Of course I can!" she smiled incredulously.

"But they can't," pointed David.

"Who?"

"Your friends."

"Ah," she smiled again. "Shall we walk towards the brook?"

"Yes." David started walking off. He turned back and offered his arm. She held it gently as they walked towards the cluster of trees. David felt that he should go home. His wife took the children away to enable him to do some work. He had not written a word in three days.

"Who are you?" he asked.

"Don't be silly!" the girl laughed. Her shoulders looked almost golden in the sunlight. She wore a beautiful long summer dress.

David decided to approach the matter more carefully. She obviously knew him. He was parched. He would love a coffee. He fumbled in his pockets and produced a cigarette. He lit it as they sat on the grass by the brook.

"What's your name?"

"Oh! Don't start again. You've had too much of that punch!" she laughed merrily. She was indeed beautiful – really beautiful.

"I'm only playing a game," he tried his luck. "Don't spoil it!"

"All right. Ursula."

"A beautiful name."

"Thank you, sir," she replied with a gently mocking inclination of her head.

"What's my name?"

"Why David of course."

"Of course..." he smiled uneasily.

"And that gentleman?"

"You're not jealous, are you?" she asked smiling.

"Desperately!" he half lied.

"What? Jealous of old Birkin? He will never lose what he feels for."

David stared at her uncomprehendingly. Ursula? Birkin? He felt light-hearted. Stupid. "He he! I've walked into a Lawrence novel." He spoke to Ursula in a sarcastic tone of voice meant to imply the depth of his game: "And one of the other two men is Gerald of course. Gudrin is there too?"

"Come on! Stop it David. It's tiresome and you've been drinking again..."

Again? David felt sleep overcoming him. He shook himself again.

This seemed very strange indeed. He was talking to a character from a novel. "He he! I am a little cartoon character. You will see a bubble over my head in a minute... I could do anything!"

He felt very keenly the stupidity of his thoughts. He had walked into a novel. That was all.

That was different from a time lapse which was an ordinary sort of experience. It was somewhat better than a temporal fourth dimension. And it certainly was more interesting than imagination – not so cheap.

"Ursula?"

"Yes David," she answered while still staring at the endless rings she had created by throwing a stone into the brook.

David felt a little cold. He could not account for it. The sun was golden and looked warm. What should he do?

What should he do?

Why is it whenever anything extraordinary appears to happen, one is never quite ready to deal with it?

Yes. Proof. He must get proof. In these cases one always seemed to go along with the events. You were being led as if in a dream. David decided to master the events – he will find out.

"Ursula?"

"Yes?"

"You know that this is only a novel," he said stupidly.

"Well, yes. I suppose it is."

"Oh!" this exclamation contained all the idiocy that the English language was capable of.

"This is Gerald's picnic?" David asked.

"Yes... Isn't your game over?"

"Where is his sister?"

"Over there with the others..."

"She will die tonight." David felt very clever. Ursula threw another stone into the brook.

"Ursula? Have you heard me? She will die tonight..."

"Don't be so horrid. I don't really like this game David... It is rather vicious." The colour rose to her cheeks and her pretty little nose dilated in an effort to control her anger. David felt that

143

he had done wrong to talk like that. He wondered if, like time travel, interference with events was not possible. Unable to resist the more childish advantages of his position he had completely overlooked the uniquely subtle overtones of this present experience. He looked at Ursula and wondered. Driven by a purely superficial curiosity he put his hand out and touched Ursula on her shoulder. She looked up and smiled.

"Stand up..." he said gently. She did and he kissed her.

"Undress..." he said.

Slowly and as if in a dream she began to take her clothes off. Her skin looked very white. David stared in amazement at her breasts as they gently fell out of her dress. He wished that he were back at home in bed. A large warm bed with Ursula. He could cover himself up to his neck and snuggle up to her back and bottom. They could talk and talk and love. If only they were in his bed.

"U – rsu – l – aaa!"

David jumped up and looked round. A man stood at a short distance from them waiting for Ursula to answer. She ran toward him holding her dress up. David gazed at her white back somehow fascinated by a minute mole on it. It was so small that he felt that it was impossible to see it at such a distance. But he did see it.

"Come back!" he shouted. She ignored him as she ran into the arms of the young man waiting for her.

David stood up feeling excited and confused. He felt intensely embarrassed at his excitement. Why had he sat there foolishly gaping at Ursula undressing? Fool! He stamped his foot and walked towards the house amidst the redness of a large luminous setting sun.

As he arrived onto the front lawn various lights started coming on. People - many more than before - were walking and laughing. He looked for Ursula. He could not see her. It was obvious that people could not see him either.

145

As he walked around the large gardens he noticed a noise that he had not heard before. A noise like the splashing of water. He followed. Several people were running away from him and into the water. Giggling, shouting and laughing, they splashed like children on a hot summer's day.

He heard Ursula's voice coming from the vast expanse of water. He was sure that this lake – or whatever it was for he could not see well in the darkening hours – was not here before. Little glimmers of light seemed to move gently across. David wondered what they were.

Boats. Little boats with a light hanging over their sides. Ursula's voice came ringing towards him from one of these boats.

Suddenly he froze.

He knew what was going to happen.

He ran towards the house which was now a mass of gleaming lights. He shouted. He screamed. He warned. No one heard him. He knew that he was wasting his time trying to warn everyone of impending death. Gerald's sister!

He ran away from the house in panic. As he reached the small brook stumbling and falling as if in a dream of the endless fall – he heard a scream coming from the lake. A woman's scream. A man's hoarse and fearful scream followed it.

David crossed the small brook and started to run. The noise behind him had stopped. He looked over his shoulder. The lights were gone. Against the black sky he could just see the outline of a large house.

"David?" he heard his wife's voice coming from the darkness. "David? Is that you?"

He was standing just outside his house in the village street. How had he covered the distance in such a short time? He smelt a pervading smell of horse manure.

147

"Is that you?"

"Yes!" whispered David.

"Oh Doady I was so worried about you..."

"What did you say?" he asked as he shut his eyes in despair.

"I said that I was..."

"No! What did you call me?"

"Call you? Doady, of course. Your child wife always calls you Doady. Naughty, naughty Doady. Jip is going to growl at you..."

From inside the kitchen David heard a loud and strong voice call, "Blossom! Blossom!"

And he shut his eyes – even harder.